Text © 2011 Giulia Belloni and Kite Edizioni S.r.l.
Illustrations © 2011 Marco Trevisan and Kite Edizioni S.r.l.
Translation © 2013 William Anselmi

Published by permission of Kite Edizioni S.r.l., Padova, Italy

Owlkids Books acknowledges the financial support of the Canada Council for the Arts, the Ontario Arts Council, the Government of Canada through the Canada Book Fund (CBF) and the Government of Ontario through the Ontario Media Development Corporation's Book Initiative for our publishing activities.

Published in Canada by
Owlkids Books Inc.
10 Lower Spadina Avenue
Toronto, ON M5V 2Z2

Published in the United States by
Owlkids Books Inc.
1700 Fourth Street
Berkeley, CA 94710

Library and Archives Canada Cataloguing in Publication

Belloni, Giulia
    Anything is possible / written by Giulia Belloni ; illustrated by Marco Trevisan.

Translation of: Tutto è possibile.
ISBN 978-1-926973-91-3

    I. Trevisan, Marco, 1984- II. Title.

PZ10.3.B45Any 2013   j853'.92   C2012-908494-8

Library of Congress Control Number: 2013930498

Manufactured in Shenzhen, Guangdong, China, in February 2013, by WKT Co. Ltd.
Job #12CB2929

A   B   C   D   E   F

 Publisher of Chirp, chickaDEE and OWL
www.owlkidsbooks.com

Anything Is Possible

Giulia Belloni ✷ Marco Trevisan

This is the story of a sheep who, from the top of her hill, watched the birds fly and thought to herself:

"How lucky they are! They can choose how
they look at things: from far away, from up close,
or from somewhere in between."

One day, the sheep had an idea and ran to see the wolf. "I have to talk to you!" she shouted.

He stopped what he was doing and listened.

"Let's build a flying machine!"

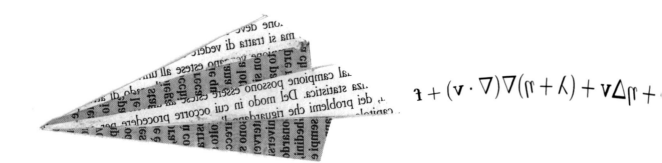

$$+ \eta \Delta \mathbf{v} + (\lambda + \eta) \nabla (\nabla \cdot \mathbf{v}) + \mathbf{f}$$

"Do you think it's that simple?! You spend too much time watching the birds in the sky," said the wolf, shaking his head.

But eventually the sheep's dream got
the better of the wolf's doubts, and they
started working on the machine together.

They gathered fabric and rods and followed the plans they had designed.

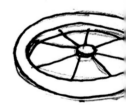

When they were ready, they started the machine and took off into the sky.

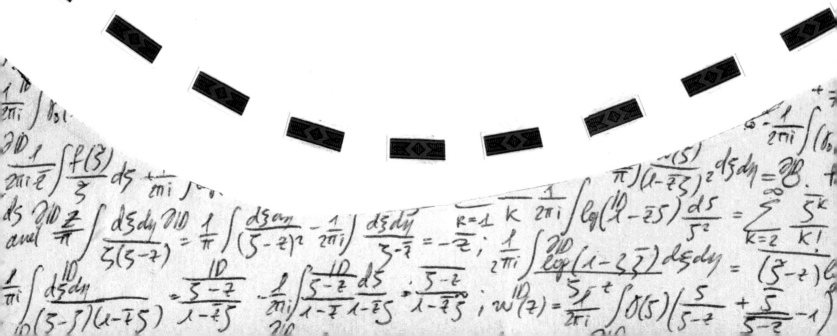

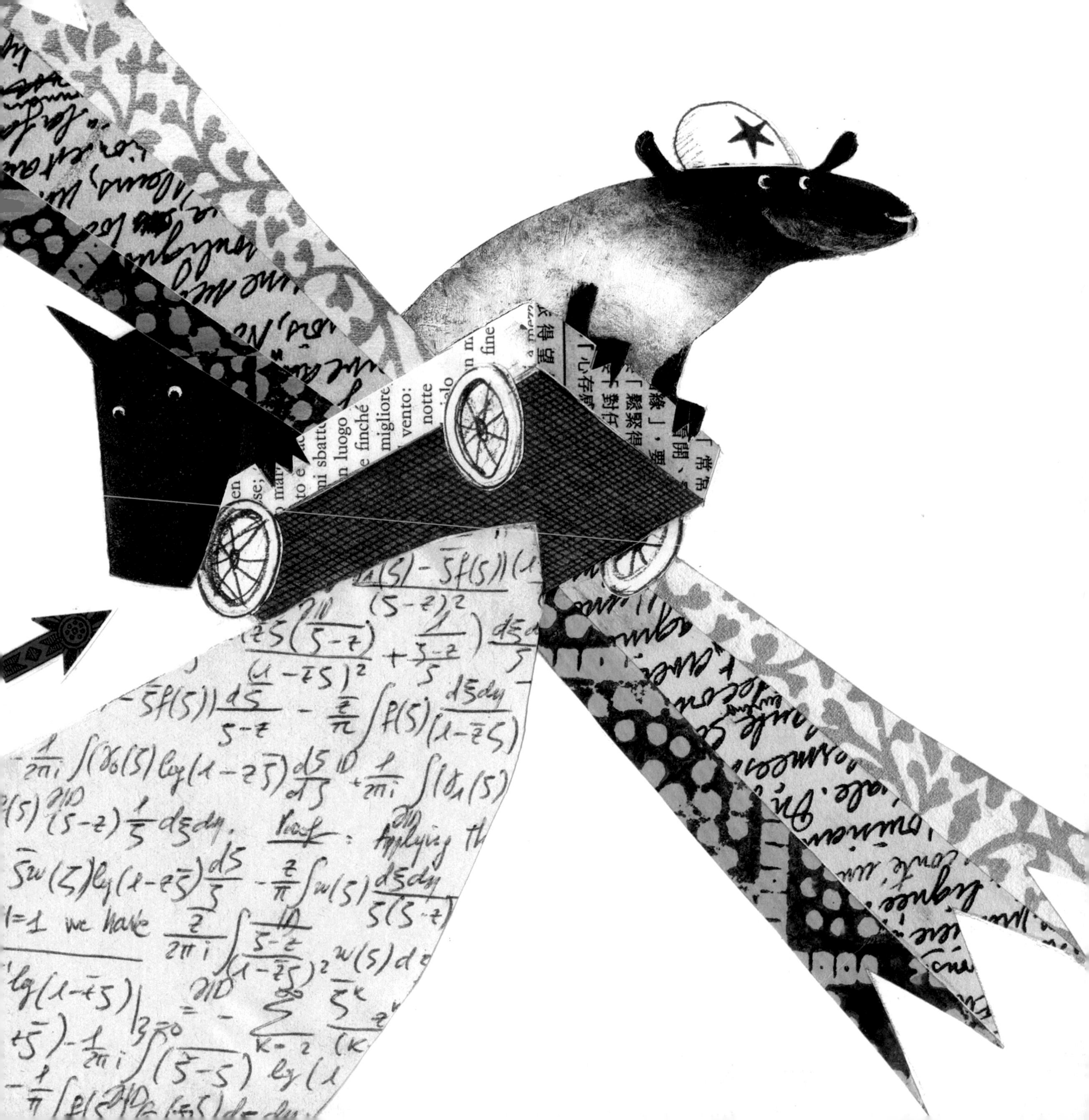

But the fabric wasn't strong enough. It soon ripped and they tumbled to the ground.

"Let's try again," said the sheep, and she blew up some balloons.

"Hold tight!" she shouted.

This time, as soon as they got the machine off the ground, birds popped the balloons.

"Oh dear!" shouted the wolf. "This is never going to work!"

But they decided to try one more time.

The sheep had a new idea. She got the wolf to cut out a dragon's tail, while she cut out a head.

This time, it worked. They were flying!

And, steadily and surely, they continued to fly.

Someone once wrote that only those who dream learn to fly.

"See?" said the sheep. "What did I tell you?"

"Anything is possible," admitted the wolf.

The sky before them was wide open.

$$\frac{d^2m}{dx^2} = -2aK\frac{d}{dx}\left[\exp\left(\frac{a}{x^2-c}\right)\left(-\frac{x}{(x^2-c)^2}\right)\right] = -2aK\left[\frac{d}{dx}\left[\exp\left(\frac{a}{x^2-c}\right)\right]\right]$$

$$Be(p). \quad S_n := \sum_{i=1}^{n} X_i \sim Bin(n,p). \quad E[S_n] = \sum_{i=1}^{n} E[X_i] = np. \quad \hat{X}_m := \frac{1}{m}S_m.$$

$$X_i \text{ iid.} \Rightarrow \frac{X_n-\mu}{\sigma}\sqrt{n} \longrightarrow N(0,1). \quad E[(X-E[X])^2] = E[X^2] + E[E[X]^2] - 2E[X]$$

$$P(-z_\alpha \le Z < z_\alpha) = 1-\alpha. \quad P\left[\hat{X}_n - z_\alpha\frac{\sigma}{\sqrt{n}} \le \mu \le \hat{X}_n + z_\alpha\frac{\sigma}{\sqrt{n}}\right] = 1-\alpha. \quad D_m(x) = \exp(a f(x))$$

$$[Df(a)]^2 + \exp(af(x)) - aD^2f(a) = \exp(af(x))\cdot a\left(aDf(a)^2 + D^2f(a)\right) = 0. \quad a = -\frac{D^2f(x)}{Df(x)^2}$$

$$\alpha^2-1 = 0 \Rightarrow t_{1,2} < 5. \quad M_\xi(a) = 0 \wedge M_\xi(b) = 0 \Rightarrow \exp(k_2/(a-\mu) - k_3) = 0 \wedge k_3-k_2$$

$$(x-\mu)\cdot x^2 + \left(\frac{b-a}{2}\right)x + \mu\cdot(\gamma=\mu)\wedge\left(a = \alpha-\beta+\mu\right)\wedge\left(b = \alpha+\beta+\mu\right) \Rightarrow \beta = \frac{b-a}{2} \Rightarrow \alpha = \frac{b+a}{2} - \mu.$$

$$(x-\mu)^2 - k_3 \longrightarrow 0. \quad h+k=1 \wedge (N^2-hN) + (hK-NK) = 2. \quad h = 1-K \quad (N=5). \quad ab=c_1$$

$$F(t) = e^t\varphi(t) \Rightarrow F'(t) = -e^t\varphi(t) + e^{-t}\varphi'(t) = e^{-t}(\varphi'(t) - \varphi(t)). \quad K = \sqrt[12]{2}. \quad (F_B/F_A) = 2s. \quad R\alpha.$$

$$\sum \mu_i(x_i - x) = 0 \quad (\mu_i > 0) \quad \alpha = \arctan\left(\frac{y}{x}\right)$$